About the Author

I've always held an ambition to write a book, and having two kids has given me lots of inspiration to make it happen. Their attempts to get up the stairs dressed in outrageous outfits, carrying the most ridiculous stuff is what led me to write this book and their exploits give me new ideas every day! Who knows, maybe I'll even get to bring another to life.

I hope this book brings a smile and its message is heard loud and clear by you and your little ones. No matter who you are, or what gets in your way, keep on climbing, you'll realise your dreams if you do.

You Can't Climb the Stairs
in a Princess Dress

YOU CAN'T CLIMB THE STAIRS
IN A *Princess* DRESS

Chris Rushbrooke

Nightingale Books

A CIP catalogue record for this title is
available from the British Library.

ISBN 978-1-83875-226-2

Nightingale Books is an imprint of
Pegasus Elliot MacKenzie Publishers Ltd.
www.pegasuspublishers.com

First Published in 2021

Nightingale Books
Sheraton House Castle Park
Cambridge England

Printed & Bound in Great Britain

Dedication

For Harriet and Ted.

Always keep climbing, my babies.

Acknowledgments

My lovely wife, Kate, for sticking by, and supporting me through everything I attempt in life.
My mum and dad for keeping me alive for thirty-five years.
Charlotte, for her wonderful illustrations.

You can't climb the stairs in a princess dress,
A young girl called Hattie tried and she got in a quite a mess.

She spilled unicorns and racing cars on every single step
And spinning tops and purple slime and a single syrupy crêpe.

You can't climb the stairs in a princess dress,
A young lad named Seb tried and it caused him some distress.

He tangled with some building blocks, his toys and his ties,
Battled with six books and pink pushchairs, what a surprise.

You can't climb the stairs in a princess dress,
There's little miss spider who resides inside a chest.

She tried to spin a web so she could navigate her way
Between the wardrobe and a fridge, a sofa and bidet.

You can't climb the stairs in a princess dress,
Gran Gran had a go, on her stairlift, button pressed.

Still, she had to dodge and duck and bob
and weave between

A load of washing Mum chucked
down to pop in the machine.

You can't climb the stairs in a princess dress,
Dad once had a go and he was really unimpressed.

He tripped over ironing, dirty nappies, Lego bricks,
Over trains, over dinosaurs and a young magician's tricks.

You can't climb the stairs in a princess dress,
A dinosaur once tried and had absolutely no success.

She jumped over dummies, massive skates, a big red pen,
Dodged a falling doll and then landed in a den.

You can't climb the stairs in a princess dress,
Just ask Mr Big Bottom with a very hairy chest.
He toppled over ice cream cones, a helmet and a sword,
He sadly lost his footing shouting,

You can't climb the stairs in a princess dress,
Just look at little Ted, look at him, oh bless.

He tried to carry all his toys at once in a big bag
But they all came crashing down, with poor Ted on top, in drag.

You can't climb the stairs in a princess dress?
Are you sure there's really no one who can do it and impress?

Who can side-step all the obstacles, the toys, the clothes, the pens?
The food and the bricks, not one can make it to the end?

YOU CAN

You CAN climb the stairs in a princess dress,
Just ask every little princess who believes in nothing less.

They can dance

and prance

and run

and jump

and make such noise so loud

SO LOUD

That their parents watch on loving, laughing, filled with joy, so proud.

Lightning Source UK Ltd.
Milton Keynes UK
UKHW050216010721
386408UK00003B/28

9 781838 752262